Lennon Bruce Fire Breather

By Kate Bartlein

For my little Dragons

STORYBOOK GENIUS PUBLISHING
sbgpublishing.com

yip jar Book Design by yipjar.com

Lennon Bruce could do something truly magical.
He could turn into a dragon.

Some days this was a wonderful thing. He liked using his scaly wings to fly across the backyard picking dandelions for his sister.

He loved using his sharp dragon claws to help mom make dinner.

He even roasted marshmallows for Shane Robbins—the one time they pretended to go camping.

Other days, turning into a dragon was not a good thing.
If something made him mad, he became a terrifying
fire-breathing monster!

Like last week, when his sister knocked over his block
tower, his face turned red, his fists clenched...and he
transformed! His hands and feet turned into
fierce claws, gigantic scaly wings
sprouted from his back, sharp
pointy teeth filled his mouth.
And then, he breathed fire!
In fact, he scorched the
whole room.

He scared his baby sister.
He even scared his dad.

Or yesterday, when Shane Robbins wouldn't let him play with the toy animals at school. Lennon turned into a fire-breathing dragon right in the middle of the classroom! His flapping wings knocked over chairs, his sharp claws ripped up paper and his fiery breath torched everything in sight.

He scared his friends.
He even scared his teacher.

To be honest, he even scared himself.

When Lennon was happy, he was the kindest,
gentlest, most helpful dragon that ever lived.

But, when he got mad...he became terrifying!
Lennon loved being a dragon, but he didn't like scaring people.

He decided to ask his mom for help with this problem.
Mom could do all sorts of magical things. She could make vegetables
taste delicious, turn ordinary blankets into the best
forts and she could even take bad dreams away.
Mom always had the best ideas.
He knew she was the right person to ask.

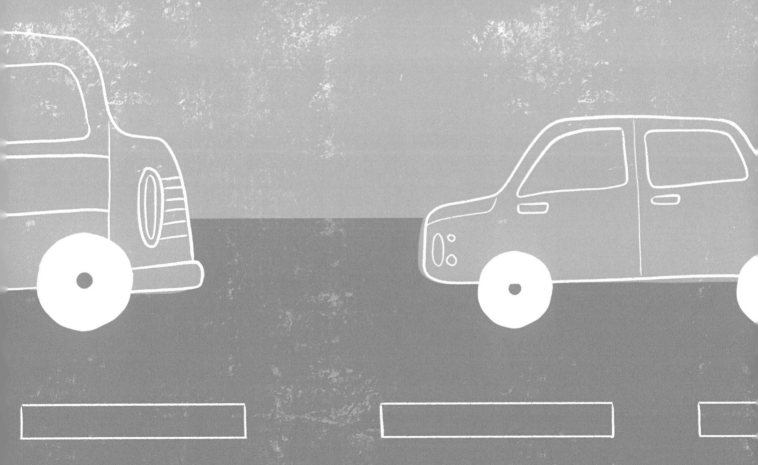

"Mom?" said Lennon.

"Yes, Lenny Bean?" she said.

"I have a problem. You know how I can turn into a dragon? I love being a dragon, but if I get mad I start breathing fire and knocking things over with my wings. I don't want to be scary."

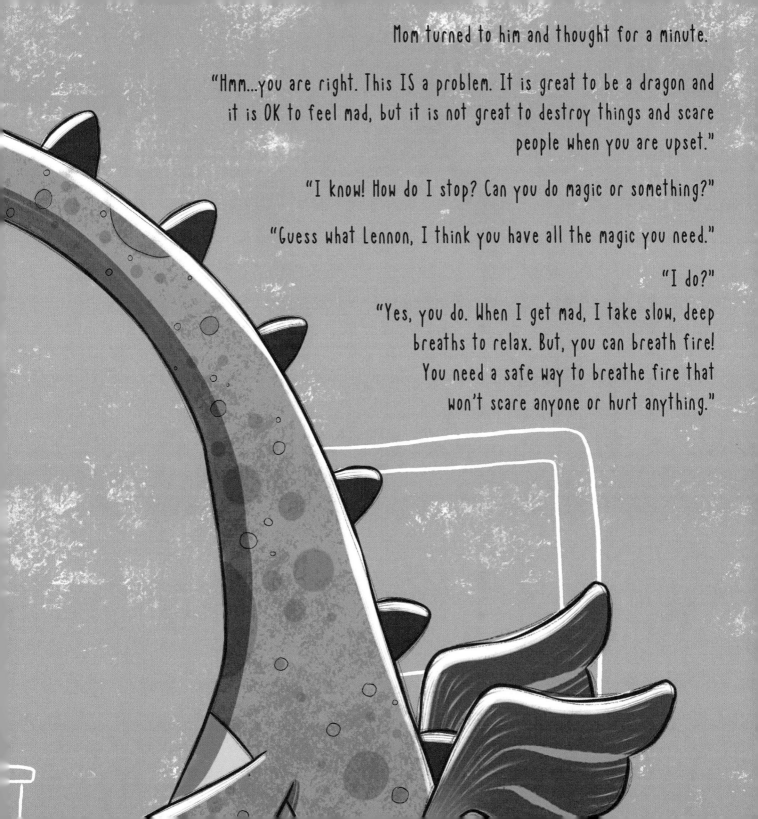

Mom turned to him and thought for a minute.

"Hmm...you are right. This IS a problem. It is great to be a dragon and it is OK to feel mad, but it is not great to destroy things and scare people when you are upset."

"I know! How do I stop? Can you do magic or something?"

"Guess what Lennon, I think you have all the magic you need."

"I do?"

"Yes, you do. When I get mad, I take slow, deep breaths to relax. But, you can breath fire! You need a safe way to breathe fire that won't scare anyone or hurt anything."

She held out her hand and spread out her five fingers.
"Look! Trees! Pretend your fingers are trees.
When you feel mad, use your fire breath to burn
down these trees—one by one until you feel calm."

Lennon stared at his fingers. He watched them grow branches
and sprout leaves. He looked back at his mom and grinned.
He thought it was an excellent plan!

Lennon spent the rest of the day happily giving his sister
dragon-back rides all over the backyard!

After dinner, Lennon was watching his favorite show when Dad suddenly turned off the TV and announced, "Time for bed, Lennon!"

Lennon felt his face turn red. His fists clenched. Scaly wings sprouted from his back, his feet turned into fierce claws and his mouth filled with pointy teeth. He was just about to torch the whole room, when he spotted Mom. She wiggled her five fingers.

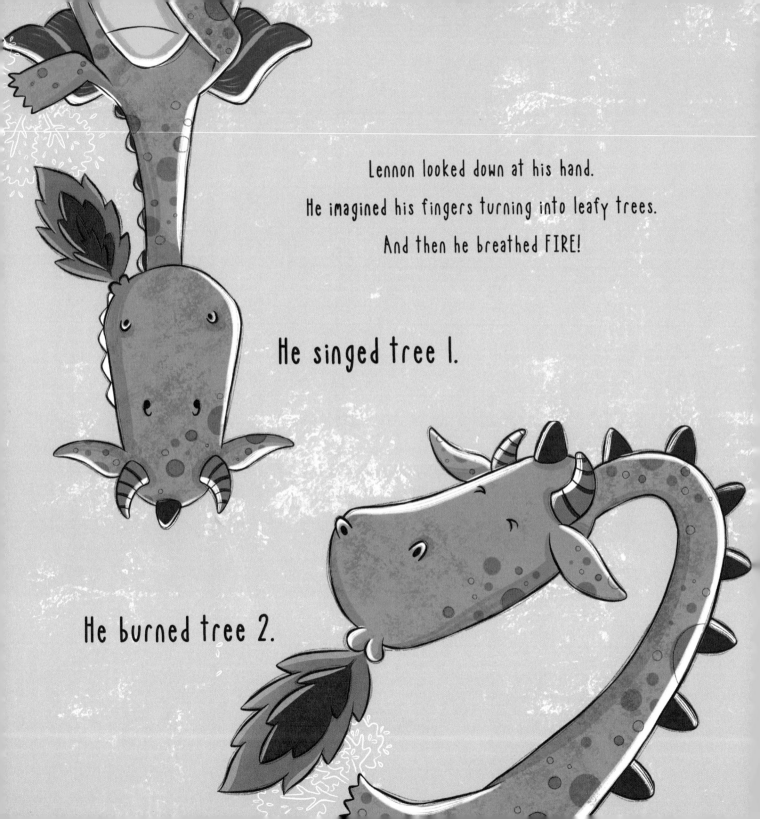

Lennon looked down at his hand.
He imagined his fingers turning into leafy trees.
And then he breathed FIRE!

He singed tree 1.

He burned tree 2.

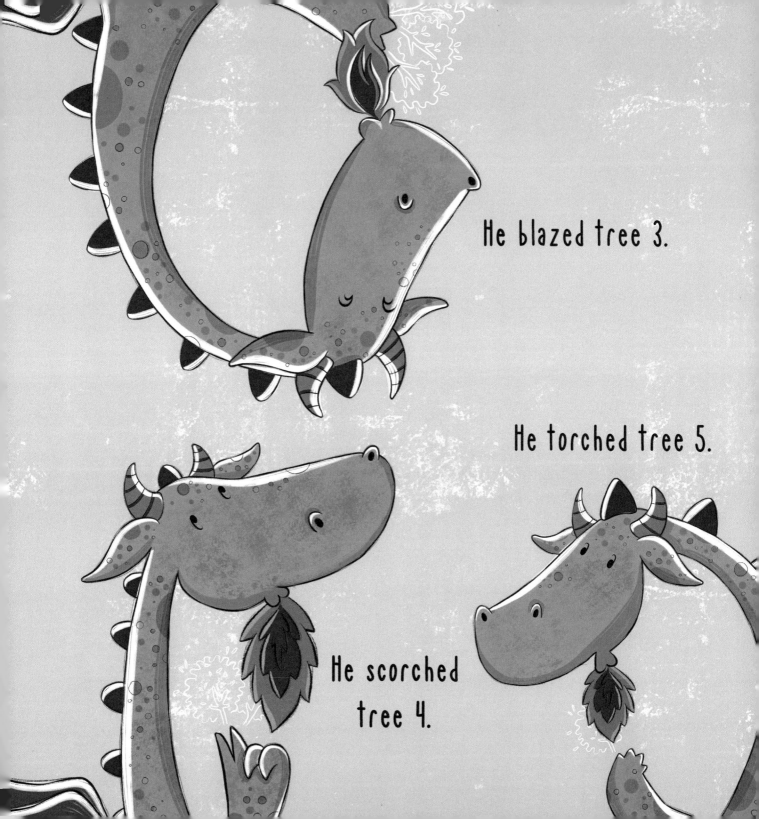

He blazed tree 3.

He torched tree 5.

He scorched tree 4.

He curled his scaly wings in close to his body and he felt calm.
It was magic!
"Dad, can I please have five more minutes?"
"Sure Lennon!" Dad grinned.

Lennon took a deep breath and imagined a puff of smoke
coming out of his mouth as he relaxed his body on the couch.
Today was a GREAT day to be a dragon!

Be a Fire Breather

Teaching children how to take deep breaths can be a great way to promote mindfulness and help them manage

BIG emotions like excitement, anger, anxiety, and sadness.

Here are a few steps to get started:

1. Use play and imagination to teach deep breathing as a coping skill.
It is always a good idea to talk about the difference between real and imaginary.
Pretending to breathe fire to calm your body down is great—playing with real fire is not.
If you or your child are uncomfortable with the tree visualization, create your own!

2. Model how to breathe in deeply through your nose and out through your mouth.
This is the way a dragon does it!

3. Give children the choice of pretending their fingers are the trees.
Each time they breathe fire put one finger down. Follow your child's lead.
Are five fire breaths enough? How about ten? Maybe one big breath blows
all the fingers down!

4. Practice when children are calm and engaged: in the car, waiting in line at the store,
before bed, or in the bathtub! That way it will be easier and feel more natural for them
to use their fire breath when they really need it.

5. Encourage their imagination by looking for other ways to practice breathing fire
(blowing bubbles, cotton balls, paper cut outs, tissues, etc).
How else can you pretend to be a dragon?

Happy Fire Breathing!

Made in the USA
Las Vegas, NV
24 March 2022

46236564R00019